THE
BAREFOOT BOOK OF
BROTHER
—— AND ——
SISTER
TALES

For Zowie, Jack, and Georgina, my god-daughter's children,
who seem to get on pretty well — M. H.

For Daniel, Melissa and Sophie, my brother and sisters – with love — E. S-S.

Barefoot Books
PO Box 95
Kingswood
Bristol
BS30 5BH

The illustrations were prepared in watercolour and mixed media on heavyweight paper
Typeset in Walbaum and Sabon
Graphic design by Design Principals, Wiltshire
Colour separation by Grafiscan, Verona
Printed and bound in Singapore by Tien Wah Press (Pte) Ltd.

This book has been printed on 100% acid-free paper

ISBN 1 84148 028 2

British Cataloguing-in-Publication Data: a catalogue record for this book is
available from the British Library

1 3 5 7 9 8 6 4 2

THE
BAREFOOT BOOK OF
BROTHER
—— AND ——
SISTER
TALES

Retold by Mary Hoffman
Illustrated by Emma Shaw-Smith

walk
the way of wonder...
Barefoot Books

CONTENTS

FOREWORD
6

HANSEL AND GRETEL

German

8

THE QUILLWORK GIRL AND HER SEVEN STAR BROTHERS

Cheyenne (North American)

16

THE RED COW

Armenian

24

ALIONUSHKA AND IVANUSHKA

Russian

32

THE GIRL WHO BANISHED
SEVEN BROTHERS

Moroccan

40

ACHOL AND MAPER

Sudanese

48

TRAMPLING THE DEMONS

Japanese

56

SOURCES

62

Foreword

If you have a brother or sister, or are raising more than one child, the chances are that you know something about both sibling rivalry and sibling friendship. Brothers and sisters often polarise, liking different things, having different circles of friends, but they are just as often very close. They can be good friends and companions, sharing each other's triumphs and setbacks. Children brought up in the same home share something very important, even though they may not realise how important it is until they are grown up.

Probably the best known story in the West about a brother and sister is 'Hansel and Gretel', which is why it is the first story in this collection. It's not the only story to explore this relationship in the material collected by the Brothers Grimm in the nineteenth century, but it is the most popular. I also wanted to include less well-known tales from other countries and to explore the brother–sister relationship from many perspectives.

Wicked stepmothers abound in these stories, as in 'Hansel and Gretel', 'The Red Cow', and 'Achol and Maper'. My deepest apologies to all readers from loving and happy reconstituted families. Remarriage, in any period before our own time, was very common as a result of women's frequent deaths in childbirth. Perhaps it was only the remarkable cases where it didn't work out that are recorded in literature.

Along with the cruel stepmother comes the jealous half-sister or half-brother. This child or children, most famously in the all-female family of Cinderella, is characterised as ugly or sickly or mean-tempered in comparison with the hero or heroine of the story. Again, this may be an attempt to console all such supplanted children with the belief that one day their goodness, innocence and inner beauty will

be rewarded and their half-siblings revealed in their true light.

In 'The Red Cow' it seems as if the half-sister is no more than a pawn in her mother's game of jealousy, but in 'Achol and Maper' the half-brothers are personally so envious of Achol's good fortune that they willingly give up both the young children to almost certain death.

Often, where there is a cruel stepmother or jealous half-sibling, there is another figure who steps in to supply the love and support which the children are missing. This is the role of the mysterious old woman in 'The Red Cow' and of the loving lion-mother in 'Achol and Maper'. The function of the wicked stepmother tradition may also be to drive the brother and sister closer together, as in 'Hansel and Gretel'.

One common theme in folk literature is that of the sister with many brothers. I have included two examples here, 'The Quillwork Girl and her Seven Star Brothers' from North America and 'The Girl who Banished Seven Brothers' from Morocco. Readers may also know the story from the Brothers Grimm of the six brothers who are turned into swans and only regain their human shapes because of the devotion of their sister. Strangely enough, I have found no instances of a story about a brother with many sisters, though it must be equally common in real life.

In most stories it seems more often the case that it is the sister who protects and rescues her brother rather than the other way round; it seems as if Hansel has all the clever ideas to begin with, but it is Gretel who finishes off the witch. In the Japanese story 'Trampling the Demons', it is the sister who helps her brother defeat the demons, even though it is the brother who bravely sets out to rescue her.

The emphasis in this collection is on equality and affection between brother and sister, rather than rivalry and discord — may this be true of all the brothers and sisters who read it.

Mary Hoffman

7

HANSEL AND GRETEL

GERMAN

There was once a poor woodcutter who lived on the edge of a deep, dark forest. He had two children by his first wife — Hansel and Gretel — but his second wife had no love for them. Times were hard where they lived and there came a day when there was nothing left to eat but a bit of bread.

'What are we to do?' groaned the woodcutter. 'I have no money to buy any more food. How are we to feed the children, let alone ourselves?'

'I have an idea,' said his wife. 'Tomorrow morning we'll take the children into the thickest part of the forest, give them a bit of bread and a fire, then leave them to Fate. They'll never find their way home and we'll have two mouths fewer to feed.'

The woodcutter was horrified. Leave his children to be eaten by wild beasts in the forest! He flatly refused but his wife nagged and nagged him until he finally gave in. But he wasn't happy about it.

Hansel and Gretel weren't happy either. There was a crack in the floorboards between their bedroom and the living room downstairs and they overheard their stepmother's wicked words — 'They'll never find their way home.' Gretel burst into tears.

'Don't worry, Gretel dear,' said Hansel. 'I have a plan of my own.'

That night, he waited until everyone was asleep. Then he crept out in the moonlight and filled his pockets with the white pebbles that surrounded the cottage.

Next morning the woodcutter and his wife led the children deep into the forest. Hansel kept stopping. He was dropping the white pebbles behind him to make a trail.

'Hurry up, boy! Why do you keep stopping?' said the stepmother, crossly.

'I am waving goodbye to my little white cat who is sitting up on the roof,' said Hansel.

'Ha, stuff and nonsense!' said the stepmother. 'That isn't your cat. It is the sun shining on the chimney.'

When they had gone a long way, the woodcutter built a large fire to keep his children warm and the stepmother gave them each a measly slice of bread for their lunch.

'We're going to chop wood now,' she said. 'We'll be back for you later.'

At first, Hansel and Gretel were quite happy. They were warm and they ate their little bit of lunch, listening to their father's axe chopping branches down somewhere nearby. But it wasn't the axe at all. The woodcutter had fastened a loose branch to a withered tree and what they could hear was the sound of it blowing back and forth in the wind.

The children fell asleep and when they woke it was already dark. The fire had burnt out and they were cold and hungry. But there was a full moon and it shone on the little white pebbles that Hansel had dropped. So the children soon found their way back home.

How their stepmother scolded them! 'Where have you been? We've been so worried about you!'

But their father was pleased to see them so they thought they were safe.

And so they were, for a while. The woodcutter sold his wood for higher prices and there was food in the larder again. But the next year, there was another great famine in the land and the woodcutter's family were down to their last half a loaf.

So the stepmother brought out her plan again. 'This time we must take them even deeper into the forest.' The woodcutter protested, but since he had given in the first time, he wasn't in a very strong position the second time.

The children overheard the plan, just as before, and Hansel tried to get some more pebbles. But this time the stepmother had locked the door; perhaps she suspected how the children had survived the last time? Gretel was desperate but her brother said, 'Don't worry — something will turn up.'

Next day, their stepmother gave them each an even smaller piece of bread. Hansel crumbled his in his pocket and stopped several times on the way to drop crumbs to mark their path.

'What is it now?' fumed the stepmother. 'You're holding us up!'

'I am only waving goodbye to my little pet dove on the roof,' said Hansel.

'Pah!' said the stepmother. 'That isn't your dove. It's only the sun glinting off the chimney!'

Deeper and deeper they went, into a part of the forest the children had never seen before. Again their father built them a good fire — it was the only thing he could do for them. Gretel shared her small crust with her brother and again they fell asleep and woke in the dark.

But this time the moon didn't shine on the breadcrumbs. The forest birds were just as hungry as the people in that country and they had swooped down and eaten every speck of bread.

Hansel and Gretel had no way of getting home so they wandered among the trees, trying to find the right path, getting more and more lost and more and more hungry.

Imagine their delight when at last they saw a little house among the trees! And when they got closer, they could see that it was made of bread and cake and sweets. The roof was built of gingerbread tiles and the windowpanes were of spun sugar. The door was made of toffee and the windowsills of thick fudge.

Hansel reached up and tore down a great chunk of gingerbread and stuffed it into his mouth. Gretel bit out a big mouthful of fudge windowsill, just where she stood. By the time they had eaten their fill, the little house looked as if it had been nibbled by an army of mice.

Just then, an old woman came hobbling out of the door. The children jumped and looked at each other guiltily. It hadn't occurred to them that the owner of the house might not want it munched by passers-by.

But the old woman didn't seem to mind. 'What pretty children!' she croaked. 'Come in, come in, do, and make yourselves at home.'

She made Hansel and Gretel delicious pancakes with sugar and apples and poured them big glasses of fresh milk. The children ate everything, in spite of all the bits of house they had already devoured. It had been so long since their stomachs had known what it was like to feel full and even longer since they had tasted any sweet luxuries.

Then the old woman showed them into a room with two comfortable beds, made up with snowy white clean sheets, and Hansel and Gretel sank gratefully into them and fell asleep.

But the children had been tricked. The owner of the gingerbread house wasn't as sweet as her home. She was really a wicked witch who liked to capture and eat children! Her plan was to fatten Hansel up and make a tasty meal out of him. As soon as he woke up, the witch bundled Hansel into a stable with bars on the door and locked him in. Then she shook Gretel awake.

'Get up, lazybones!' she shouted, no longer the kind old woman of the day before. 'Your brother's in the stable and I want him fattened up. Fetch some water and cook him a meal that will put more flesh on his bones.'

Every day the witch bossed Gretel about and gave her nothing but

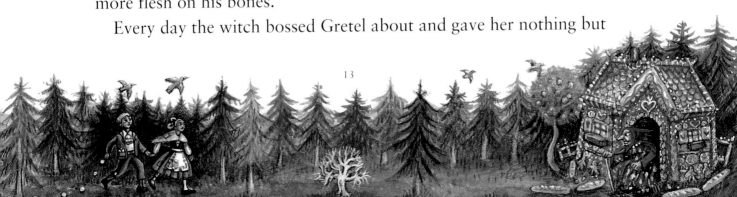

crab-shells to eat. But Hansel got roast chicken and potatoes and gravy and stuffing, and apple stir-up and jam roly-poly and treacle pudding. He was indeed getting quite plump but every day, when the witch came to the stable door and said, 'Give me your finger to feel, so I can see if you're fat enough to eat,' he stuck out a chicken bone. And the witch, who had very poor eyesight, couldn't believe how skinny his finger felt.

After a month, she lost patience. 'Build up the fire and fetch a big pot of water,' she told Gretel. 'I'm going to boil that brother of yours, fat or thin.' Gretel did as she was told, her mind racing to think of a way to save Hansel.

'We'll bake some bread to have with him,' said the witch, 'while the water boils. I've heated the oven and made the dough. Why don't you creep into the oven and see if it's hot enough?' She meant to slam the oven door on Gretel and bake her too, such a wicked old witch was she.

But Gretel was so clever she pretended to be stupid. 'What do you mean?' she asked the witch. 'I don't see how I could get in there.'

'Oh, useless girl!' grumbled the witch. 'Do I have to show you myself? It's perfectly easy. See, you just open the door and creep in like this...'

SLAM! In a trice, Gretel had pushed the witch all the way into the oven and shut the door tight on her. She was burned to a crisp.

Gretel ran to her brother's prison and let him out. How they hugged and kissed for joy! It was safe to go back into the witch's house now and they helped themselves to lots of jewels and gold coins which they found in big wooden chests in a back room. (Gretel helped herself to some more windowsill and a big chunk of

door too, but Hansel couldn't eat another morsel.)

They set off to find their way home and it still wasn't easy. They came to a river, too wide to wade across. Swimming on it was a big white duck.

'Let's ask the duck to take us across,' said Hansel.

'Not both of us at once,' said Gretel. 'You weigh a good deal more than you used to.'

But the duck was happy to take them over together. And once they were on the far bank, the children recognised where they were. They ran the rest of the way home.

They found the woodcutter sitting sadly on his own. He jumped up in amazement when he saw the son and daughter he had given up for lost long ago. He told them that their stepmother was dead and I can't pretend they were at all sad to hear it.

'Look what we have brought back, Father,' said Gretel, and she emptied all the jewels out of her knotted apron. When Hansel had added the treasure from his pockets, the family had enough to make sure that their larder was never empty for the rest of their days.

But somehow, Hansel and Gretel had lost their taste for sweet things and they never ate gingerbread again.

THE QUILLWORK GIRL AND HER SEVEN STAR BROTHERS

CHEYENNE (NORTH AMERICAN)

Hundreds of years ago, among the Cheyenne people of North America, there lived a girl who was highly skilled at quillwork. She invented her own designs, which were vividly coloured and elaborate, and she decorated all sorts of different things — clothes, quivers for holding arrows, even whole tipis.

She became famous for miles around for the quality and beauty of her work and everyone called her the Quillwork Girl. One day, the girl was sitting in her parents' lodge and she started to make a complete outfit for a man. It was made of white buckskin and she decorated every piece of it — the shirt, leggings, moccasins — with her wonderful quillwork.

Her mother was a little puzzled, because the girl had no brothers, nor did she have a boyfriend. 'So why is she making a man's suit?' thought the mother, but she didn't say anything.

It took months for the girl to finish making the wonderful suit. But as soon as she had finished it, she started making another. And another. She worked for a whole year and by the end of it she had made six full-size suits and one small one. There never was a collection of clothes like it and no Cheyenne had ever worn anything half as splendid.

For the whole year, the girl's mother had bitten back her questions and never asked her daughter who the clothes were for. Her patience was rewarded for, when she had finished the seventh suit, the small one, the girl spoke to her mother and said, 'Somewhere, many days' walk from here, live seven brothers. I have never had any brothers and I want to make them mine. I have made these clothes for them and everyone who sees my brothers wearing them will be filled with admiration.'

'I will go with you, my daughter,' said her mother.

'But it is a long way, Mother,' said the girl.

'Then I shall go as far as I can,' said her mother.

They wrapped up the decorated suits and tied the seven bundles to their strongest dogs and set out northwards.

'You seem to know the way,' said the mother.

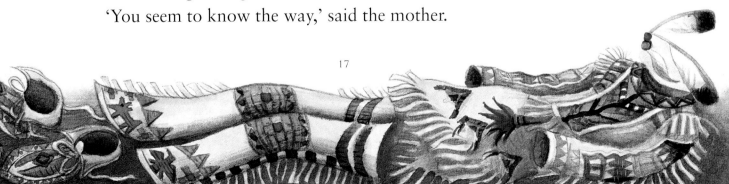

'I do,' said the girl. 'I know where the seven young men live and much else about them. But don't ask me how I know, for I cannot answer. I really have no idea.'

The mother walked as far as she could, but at last she turned back south and left the girl to carry on northwards. The girl walked and walked until she reached a broad stream. Beside it was a large painted tipi. The girl waded across the stream, which was very shallow so that the dogs got only their legs wet and the bundles stayed dry.

She stood outside the tipi and called.

'I am here, the girl-who-looks-for-brothers, and I bring you presents.'

Out of the tipi stepped a young boy of about ten years old.

'Welcome,' he said. 'I've been expecting you. I am the youngest of seven brothers, but the others are all out hunting the buffalo.'

'Are they expecting me, too?' asked the girl.

'No,' said the boy. 'They don't have my special gift of knowing, nor my other special gifts.'

'What special gifts are those?' asked the girl.

'You will find out in good time,' said the boy.

Then the girl unpacked her bundles and sent the dogs home. She gave the boy the smallest suit and he put it on. It fitted him perfectly and was the finest he had ever worn.

'I shall be happy to be your brother,' he said.

'And I shall happily be sister to all seven of you,' said the girl.

The boy showed her into the tipi, where there were seven beds. The girl laid out a white buckskin suit on each of the six biggest beds. Then she unpacked her own bundle and set to work to make a meal.

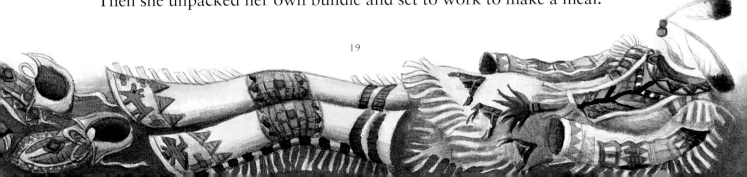

As evening fell, the six brothers returned. They saw their little brother dressed in his splendid buckskin suit, decorated with colourful quillwork.

'Where did that fine outfit come from?' they asked.

'Our sister made it for me,' said the boy. 'She has made some outfits for you too. And she has made supper. Come and meet her!'

The brothers were delighted with their new sister. They all put on their fine clothes and promised to look after and provide for the girl ever afterwards.

A few days later, when the older brothers were again out hunting, a young buffalo calf came and tapped with its hoof at the tipi. The boy went out and asked the calf what it wanted.

'I have been sent by the buffalo nation,' said the calf. 'We have heard of your beautiful sister, the Quillwork Girl, and we want her to live with us.'

'Certainly not,' said the boy. 'Go away!'

'Very well,' said the calf. 'But someone bigger than me will come and ask for her.'

The next day a heifer came and snorted outside the tipi.

'What do you want?' asked the boy.

'I have been sent by the buffalo nation,' said the heifer. 'We want your beautiful sister, the Quillwork Girl.'

'You can't have her,' said the boy. 'Go away!'

'Then someone bigger than me will come,' said the heifer and galloped off.

On the third day, a large buffalo cow grunted and pawed the ground outside the tipi.

'I am sent by the buffalo nation,' said the cow. 'Give me your

sister, the Quillwork Girl.'

'No!' said the boy, though he had to stand on tiptoe to talk to the cow. 'You can't have her. Go away!'

'Then someone very big indeed will come,' said the cow. 'And he won't be alone. If you don't give him the Quillwork Girl, he will kill you all.'

The next day all the brothers stayed at home. They felt the earth beneath the tipi begin to tremble, then they heard a terrible rumbling getting nearer and louder. They looked outside and there, in the distance, was the biggest buffalo bull they had ever seen. Behind him came the whole buffalo nation, bellowing and snorting.

When the whole buffalo nation was pawing the ground outside

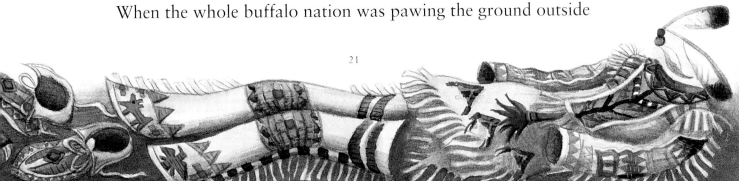

the tipi, the youngest brother stepped out and asked coolly, 'Giant buffalo, what do you want?'

'Your sister,' said the bull. 'Give me the Quillwork Girl or I shall kill you.'

The boy went into the tipi and brought out the girl and his six brothers.

'Hand her over,' snorted the bull.

'No,' said the boy. 'She doesn't want to go with you.'

'Then prepare to die!' roared the bull and lowered his massive head to charge.

'Quick!' said the boy. 'Up this tree!'

They all climbed the nearest tree and the boy shot an arrow into its trunk before joining them. Immediately the tree grew a thousand feet in the air, taking the seven brothers and the Quillwork Girl with it.

Now, it takes longer to read about it than it did to do and the buffalo bull ran straight into the tree-trunk and gave himself a headache. He was furious!

'I'll chop the tree down with my horns!' he roared and he charged at the trunk again.

The Quillwork Girl and her seven brothers looked down at all the buffaloes milling round the tree. The youngest brother fired another arrow into the trunk and the tree shot up another thousand feet.

Again the bull charged the trunk with all the power of a battering ram, and the tree shook, so the boy fired another arrow. Up they went again but this time, when the bull charged, they nearly fell out of the branches.

'Hold on!' cried the boy and fired his last arrow. This time the tree shot up above the clouds.

'Quick! Step out on to the clouds,' the boy told his sister and brothers. They stepped fearfully off the branches and found that the clouds supported them as well as the earth had done. And as soon as they had left it, the tree toppled under the final onslaught of the enraged bull.

They looked down as the huge tree fell to earth, knowing they could not get back.

'What shall we do, little brother?' asked the brothers, but the Quillwork Girl was not afraid. She realised that her youngest brother had very special gifts indeed.

'Don't worry,' said the boy. 'I'll turn us all into stars.'

At once, they were bathed in a bright light. They stepped off the clouds and formed themselves into the pattern that some people call the Big Dipper. You can still see them in the sky today. The very bright star that they point to is the Quillwork Girl, who fills the heavens with her beautiful designs, and the twinkling star at the end of the dipper's handle is the youngest brother.

THE RED COW

ARMENIAN

There once was a shepherd who was not very rich, but he was happy. He had a wife he loved, a son and a daughter and, as well as his flock of sheep, one very good red cow. The cow gave creamy milk for all the shepherd's family to drink and his children grew tall and strong.

But his wife became ill with a sickness that even the red cow's milk could not cure. She took to her bed and died. The shepherd was very sad, but he was also worried about his children. He had to be out of doors all day looking after his sheep and soon ran out of friends and neighbours to watch out for his son and daughter.

So he married again, for the sake of having someone to look after the children. Maybe his second wife knew that was why he married her and maybe that was why she was so mean to them. And she was mean, very mean. She would give them only stale crusts to eat. The children lost their healthy glow and started to grow thin.

The shepherd realised he had made a terrible mistake.

'Why do you treat them so badly?' he asked his wife. 'They have done nothing to you.'

'I didn't ask to have them,' said his wife. 'Why should I look after them?'

In the end, their stepmother was so cruel to the children that their father started to send them out to take care of the sheep while he stayed at home. It was hard work looking after the sheep, protecting them from wolves, making sure they didn't stray or fall into a ditch, and rounding them up every evening to bring back to their pen, but there was someone to help the children — the red cow. She took pity on them, remembering the happy times they used to have.

'Rest, little ones,' she mooed. 'I'll tend the sheep while you play.'

And when the time came for them to eat their pathetic little crusts, the cow came and fed them her rich creamy milk, just as in the old days.

In time, the shepherd's second wife had a baby girl of her own. She was as devoted to her daughter as she was hateful to her stepchildren. And she couldn't understand why the older two grew big and strong on the crusts she gave them, while her own daughter stayed sickly and weak in spite of being given delicious freshly baked bread.

When the little girl was old enough, she was sent out to join her brother and sister in the fields. She saw them drinking the red cow's milk and wanted some for herself. Well, the red cow did not mind, but although her milk tasted good to the two older children, it seemed bitter as vinegar to the little girl.

The shepherd's wife could not understand why her daughter stayed undersized and scrawny while her stepchildren flourished.

'What do they get to eat that you don't?' she questioned the girl. 'You have four or five loaves a day and I give them only crusts, yet they grow like weeds. They must have some other food.'

'They have the milk from the red cow, Mother,' said the girl. 'But I get that too. Only they say it tastes like honey to them, while it seems more like mustard to me.'

'The red cow!' exclaimed the woman. 'That must be it!' She was always jealous and suspicious about any part of her husband's life that belonged to the time before she married him. She decided to get rid of the cow. Next morning she said to her husband. 'I have had a dream which explains why our daughter is so sickly. A holy man appeared to me and told me it was that red cow's fault. We must have her killed.'

'Killed?' exclaimed the shepherd. 'But what would we do for milk and cheese?'

He was very fond of the red cow but his wife got her way in the end. The cow heard him sharpening a knife and knew what was going to happen to her. When the children came to feed her, there were tears in her eyes.

'What is the matter, dear Rosie?' asked the girl.

'I am going to be killed,' said the cow. 'It is your stepmother's decision. But I'm not crying for myself, only that I have to leave you.'

'Let us go and plead with her,' said the boy. 'We'll beg her to let you live.'

'No,' said the cow. 'She would only beat you and treat you even worse than she does already. But there is something you can do. It

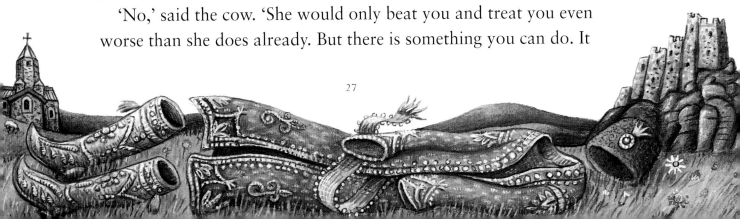

will be hard but remember it's what I want. When I have been killed, get hold of some of my blood and smear it on your faces. Then you will always have a golden glow about you. After they have cooked me, gather up my bones and hooves and hide them in the manger in my shed. And one last thing — cut off one of my horns and whenever you feel hungry suck on it and you will feel full and satisfied.'

The children were very sad, but they trusted their friend the red cow. 'Only, who will look after us?' they asked. The red cow took them to a cave in the hills and introduced them to an old woman who lived there. She promised to look out for them when the red cow was dead.

Everything happened the way the cow had described. She was killed. The children secretly smeared their faces with her blood, weeping quietly for their friend. Their stepmother cooked the meat from the cow and gave some to her daughter. It tasted just like straw to her. Then the woman gave some of the stew to her stepchildren. (She wouldn't normally give them meat but she knew they loved the red cow and it was a new way of being cruel to them.) The children ate the stew and to them it tasted sweet as honeycomb.

After that, the stepmother gave up feeding them altogether. Whenever they were hungry they went to the manger in the barn and sucked on the red cow's horn. Then they felt as full as if they had eaten a proper meal.

That winter, the whole family was invited to a royal wedding. The woman made her husband buy grand clothes for their daughter, but the older children had to stay at home. When the others had left for the party, the voice of the red cow was heard mooing from the shed. The old woman heard it and came down from her cave to see what was going on.

'Lift the slab under the manger,' said the red cow's voice, 'and you will find clothes fine enough for my friends to go to the wedding.'

So the old woman and the boy and girl — who were really a young man and woman by now — lifted the slab and found the most wonderful outfits hidden underneath. Silk and satin they were, trimmed with lace and embroidered with jewels. There was a pair of silver slippers for the girl and a pair of gold boots for the boy.

Dressed in all their finery, they went to the wedding. Their stepmother didn't recognise them. 'What a handsome pair,' she gushed to her husband. 'Wouldn't it be a fine thing if that young man wanted to marry our daughter?'

But the young man danced with all the other beautiful young

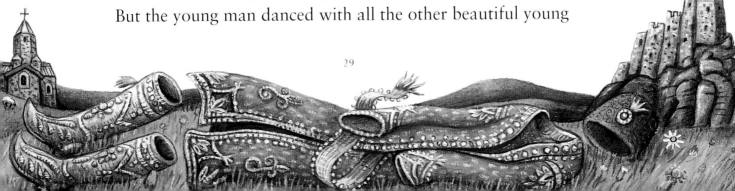

women and not with his half-sister. His real sister danced with the prince and they both seemed to enjoy it.

At the end of the party, the young pair left before their family and changed back into their ragged clothes. But the girl had lost one of her silver slippers.

The next day, their stepmother was full of stories about the wedding-party. 'There were two such fine young people there,' she told them. 'The same age as you, but otherwise you have nothing else in common. They were so elegant and well-dressed! I'm sure the young woman will marry the prince. And if the young man were to marry my daughter, just think! We'd be related to royalty!'

Just then there was a knock at the door. It was the king's messenger. The prince had found a silver slipper in the palace grounds and was anxious to find the owner.

'Are there any young ladies in this house who were at the party?' asked the messenger. 'If so, they should try this slipper on.'

Well, of course, the stepmother was delighted and rushed upstairs to fetch her daughter. But first she pushed the other girl and her brother out of the door, saying, 'Get back to your sheep.

This is court business and needn't concern you!'

The shoe did not fit the girl, of course. From the fields, the boy and his sister watched the messenger leave and as he passed the shed, they heard the voice of the red cow, saying, 'Wait! There is another young woman. Tell the prince to expect her this evening.'

That evening, the old woman from the cave came down and dressed the young people in their fine clothes again, and they went to the palace where the girl tried on the silver slipper and showed the prince its matching partner.

'This is the woman I shall marry,' said the prince, much against his father's will. But the prince knew his own mind and another royal wedding took place before too long.

The young people lived at the palace in great comfort, eating all the best food and wearing fine clothes every day. The prince sent for the shepherd to live with them but the unkind stepmother and her scrawny daughter had to stay and mind the sheep.

The princess and her brother buried the remains of the red cow in the palace gardens with great honour and never forgot the friend who had looked after them when they had nothing.

ALIONUSHKA AND IVANUSHKA

RUSSIAN

Once upon a time there was a king and a queen. They had a daughter called Alionushka and a son called Ivanushka. Alionushka was the older of the two and took good care of her little brother. Then the king and queen died and the children had no one to look after them, so they wandered the world together looking for a new way of life.

They came to a cattle-pond and Ivanushka said, 'I am so thirsty, Sister. I must drink.'

'Oh no, Ivanushka,' said his sister. 'If you drink from the cattle-pond you will turn into a calf.'

So Ivanushka did not drink.

Then they came to a field of horses, with a water-trough in it.

Ivanushka said, 'I am so, so thirsty, Sister. I must drink.'

'No, Ivanushka,' said his sister. 'If you drink from the horse-trough, you will turn into a colt.'

So Ivanushka did not drink.

Then they came to a lake with sheep grazing around it.

Ivanushka said, 'I am really thirsty, Sister. I must drink.'

'No, Ivanushka,' said his sister. 'If you drink from the lake, you will become a lamb.'

So Ivanushka did not drink.

Further on they travelled and found a stream with pigs feeding beside it.

'I am terribly thirsty,' said Ivanushka. 'I really must drink.'

'No, Ivanushka,' said his sister. 'If you drink from the stream, you will become a piglet.'

So Ivanushka did not drink.

They walked a long way further and came to a well with a flock of goats grazing nearby.

'Sister, Sister,' said Ivanushka. 'I am parched. Please let me drink.'

'No, Ivanushka,' said his sister. 'If you drink from the well, you will become a kid.'

But Ivanushka could not help himself. He drank from the well.

As soon as he had slaked his thirst, Ivanushka began to shrink. His curly hair turned white and spread all over his body. He sank on to all fours and sprouted horns and a small tail.

'Maa-ka-ka,' he bleated. Ivanushka had become a kid.

Alionushka wept for her little brother. She took her silken belt from round her waist and tied it round the kid's neck. Still crying softly, she walked on, the kid pulling ahead on his silken lead.

The kid ran on, dragging Alionushka into the garden of a certain king. There the little goat started to eat the cabbages. The servants ran to the king to tell him that a beautiful young woman was in his garden with a kid on a silken lead.

The king was intrigued and summoned Alionushka to tell him her story.

'The king my father and the queen my mother both died,' said Alionushka. 'We children remained. I am a princess and my little brother Ivanushka is a prince.'

'And where is your brother now?' asked the king.

Alionushka pointed to the kid.

'Here is Ivanushka,' she said. 'He drank from a well where goats had drunk before him, although I warned him what would happen. And now he is a kid but I still love him dearly.'

And she cried more tears, while the little white kid butted his head against her face to comfort her.

The king was entranced. Alionushka was beautiful and a princess, too. And her story was so moving. He fell in love with her on the spot and they were married not long after.

For a long time the king and queen and the kid lived happily together. The kid ate his meals with them and walked with them in the garden and wore a golden collar, since he couldn't wear a prince's crown.

One day the king went out hunting and, while he was away, a sorceress came and cast a spell over Queen Alionushka. She fell ill and grew pale and thin. Everything in the castle seemed to share in the queen's sickness. The flowers in the gardens withered and the vegetables shrivelled. The grass dried up and the trees drooped. Everything looked thirsty.

When the king returned from hunting, he was shocked.

'My dear, are you sick?' he asked.

'Yes, I am sick,' answered his queen, in a small voice, but the

next day she encouraged him to go hunting again. And while the king was away, the sorceress slipped into the castle, disguised as a healing-woman. She persuaded the servants to admit her to the queen's bedchamber and said, 'If you want to get well, you must go to the sea at twilight and drink the salt water.'

So Alionushka went to the sea, with the kid trotting beside her.

He seemed very uneasy and, as Alionushka went down to the water's edge, it was his turn to cry, 'No, Alionushka, do not drink!' But all that came out was 'Maa-ka-ka!'

The sorceress leapt out from behind a rock and grabbed Alionushka. She tied a stone around her neck and threw her into the sea.

Alionushka sank to the bottom of the sea and the kid ran to the water's edge, bleating and crying.

The sorceress turned herself into the very image of Alionushka and went back to the castle.

That night, when the king came back from his hunting, he was so pleased to see his wife looking better that he didn't notice that the gardens were still dry and lifeless.

The king and the false queen sat down to supper and she ordered the door to be shut.

'Where is the kid?' asked the king. 'Does your brother not dine with us tonight?'

'He has a rather goat-like smell,' said the false queen. 'It puts me off my food.'

The next day, when the king was out hunting, the sorceress threatened the kid. 'As soon as the king returns, I shall ask him to give orders for you to be killed.' And she did.

36

The king was full of pity for the kid. He was, after all, the queen's brother. But the queen seemed quite determined.

'I am tired of him,' she said. 'He annoys me.'

So the orders were given and knives sharpened. The kid ran to the king and said, 'Let me go down to the sea and clean my insides by drinking sea-water.'

The king could understand him and gave him permission, so the kid ran down to the sea's edge and called out,

Sister Alionushka, come to me.
Rise up from your prison in the
    sea.
The butcher sharpens up his
    knife.
I'm to be killed, says the
    king's new wife.

And the voice of Alionushka replied,

Little brother, I may not
    rise.
The stone about my neck
    still lies.
I would save you if I might,
But it keeps me in my plight.

The kid wept and went back to the castle. But later in the day he again asked the king's permission to go down to the sea. He couldn't believe his big sister would not save him.

Again he called out,

Sister Alionushka, come to me.
Rise up from your prison in the sea.
The butcher sharpens up his knife.
I'm to be killed, says the king's new wife.

And the voice of Alionushka replied again,

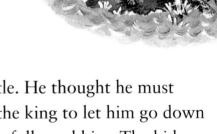

Little brother, I may not rise.
The stone about my neck still lies.
I would save you if I might,
But it keeps me in my plight.

The kid went weeping back to the castle. He thought he must certainly die, but one last time he asked the king to let him go down to the sea and, this time, the king secretly followed him. The kid went down to the shore bleating piteously,

Sister Alionushka, come to me.
Rise up from your prison in the sea.
The butcher sharpens up his knife.
I'm to be killed, says the king's new wife.

And the king heard the voice of Alionushka reply,

Little brother, I may not rise.
The stone about my neck still lies.
I would save you if I might,
But it keeps me in my plight.

But this time her great love for her
brother made her strain against
the weight of the stone and
she struggled to the surface.
When the king saw
Alionushka's beloved face
rising up all wet through the
waves, he rushed into the sea and lifted her out. He cast
the stone away and embraced her joyfully as the kid capered
around them.

Alionushka told him everything that had happened. When they
got back to the castle, the garden was blooming again and the
sorceress was running away, but the king caught her and ordered
her to be burned to death. And as soon as the sorceress had burned
to ashes, the white kid stood on his hind legs and stretched his arms
and became a young man again, Prince Ivanushka. (He looked very
strange in his golden collar, until it was cut off and turned into a
crown.)

So Alionushka and Ivanushka lived happily ever after with the
king in his castle in the middle of gardens filled with flowers.

THE GIRL WHO BANISHED SEVEN BROTHERS

MOROCCAN

There was once a woman who had seven sons in a row. Healthy boys, they were, and handsome and she loved them dearly. But every time her labour pains began, she hoped in her heart for a little daughter.

Time passed and the woman expected another child. Her seven sons were as eager for a sister as she was for a daughter. But on the day the baby was due, the seven brothers had to go out to hunt as usual.

Their father's sister had come to help with the birth, so the young men said to her, 'If the baby is a girl, hang a spindle from the door-post. We shall see it from far off and spin round and come straight back home.'

'And what if it's another boy?' asked their aunt.

'Then hang up a sickle and we shall cut loose and never come home again.'

The woman's time came and she gave birth to a little girl at last. She was very happy with her little daughter.

So was the aunt. She had never liked her nephews, so she thought to herself, 'This is my chance to be rid of them,' and she hung a sickle out, even though a girl had been born.

From a distance, the brothers saw it and cursed their luck. 'Another boy!' they said. 'It's time for us to go.' And they directed their feet away from home and towards the desert.

When her brothers failed to return, the girl's parents named her Wudei'a, which was short for 'the girl who banished seven'. It seems that little Wudei'a never wondered about her strange name until she was fifteen years old. She was playing with some friends when they fell out over their game, as often happens, and one of the girls said to her, 'What can we expect from you? You're the one whose seven brothers ran away into the desert when you were born!'

Wudei'a was appalled. She ran home and asked her mother, 'Do I really have seven brothers?'

Her mother sighed and told her the whole story. 'Seven brothers you had, as strong and well-built as any young men ever seen. But the day you were born, they disappeared into the desert and, to our great sorrow, we have never heard a word about them since.'

'Then I shall go and find them,' said Wudei'a.

'How?' asked her mother. 'After fifteen years, the trail is cold.'

'I don't know,' said Wudei'a. 'But I shall search the four corners of the earth till I discover them — and I shall bring them home.'

Her mother gave her a camel and a maidservant and manservant to accompany her and Wudei'a set out into the desert. But after they were out of sight of the village, the manservant made Wudei'a get off the camel and put the maid up in her place. They had a plan to deceive the seven brothers if ever they found them.

They travelled in this way for three days, with the maid riding in comfort and poor Wudei'a walking till her feet bled. Then they met a merchant's caravan. 'Have you seen seven young men out hunting together?' asked the manservant.

'Seven such young men live together in that castle over there,' answered the merchant.

When the merchant was out of sight, the manservant heated up some pitch and smeared it all over Wudei'a's skin so that she looked black from top to toe. Then they all went to the castle and knocked at the gate.

'Behold!' said the manservant, when the brothers came to greet him. 'Here is your sister,' he said, pointing to the maid. 'Here is your mother's eighth and last child.'

At first the brothers didn't believe him. 'But our mother had another son,' they said. 'That's why we left home.'

But after a while the brothers accepted the servant's story and made the maid welcome as their sister. Of course, they also believed that Wudei'a was her maid.

The next day, the brothers decided to stay at home with their sister instead of going hunting. The oldest brother said to Wudei'a, 'Come, girl, and comb my hair.'

Wudei'a took up the comb and ran it through her brother's hair. She was so overwhelmed by her situation that she started to weep

softly. A tear fell on her arm and rubbed away some of the pitch. Immediately, the brother was suspicious. 'Tell me why you are disguised,' he said.

Wudei'a told him the whole story. Her brother ordered a sweet-scented bath to be poured for her and a clean soft robe to be laid out for her, and then went off to order the two servants to be put to death.

All seven brothers were delighted with their real sister and made a great fuss of her. But after a few days, they needed to go hunting again.

They said, 'Sister, lock the castle gate and don't open it till we return in seven days. Lock the cat in with you and take care of her. And of everything you eat, you must give her half.'

Wudei'a did as she was advised and seven days later her brothers returned. They were pleased to see her safe and well.

'As long as you do what we say, you will be safe here,' they said. 'After all, there are seven doors to your room, six of wood and the seventh of iron. And remember to give half of everything you eat to the cat. She and our pet dove are the only ones who know where our hunting grounds are.'

The next time the brothers went hunting, Wudei'a was sweeping the floor when she found a broad bean. Without thinking, she popped it into her mouth.

'What are you eating?' asked the sharp-eyed cat.

'Nothing,' said Wudei'a. 'Only a bean I found on the floor.'

'Then why didn't you give half the bean to me?' said the cat. 'It will be the worse for you.'

And the cat went and put out the fire by peeing on it. Now Wudei'a could not cook any food. She managed on cold and raw food for a few days, and then she could stand it no longer. She went out of the castle at night-time and followed a light she could see in the desert.

It came from a cooking-fire and Wudei'a meant to ask the owner for some embers to take home. But the fire belonged to a desert-demon and he would as soon have cooked Wudei'a over his fire

than given her a bit to take away! But it happened that he was feeling full at the time so he gave her the fire and let her go home. When he had slept off his meal, however, he followed her footprints in the sand back to the castle. The demon soon broke the lock on the castle gate and went to the girl's room. Outside her door he sang,

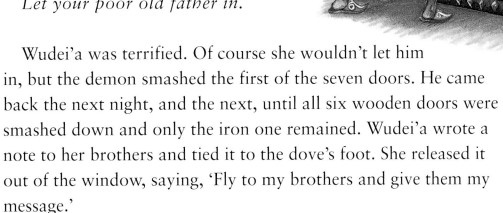

Wudei'a, Wudei'a, who banished her
  brothers,
Show more mercy to another.
Don't commit a second sin.
Let your poor old father in.

Wudei'a was terrified. Of course she wouldn't let him in, but the demon smashed the first of the seven doors. He came back the next night, and the next, until all six wooden doors were smashed down and only the iron one remained. Wudei'a wrote a note to her brothers and tied it to the dove's foot. She released it out of the window, saying, 'Fly to my brothers and give them my message.'

The dove flew through the desert until it found the brothers' hunting ground. It landed on the oldest brother's shoulder and he recognised it. He read the message:

Six doors are broken; the iron one remains.
Come quickly if you want to see your sister again.

45

So the brothers hurried back to the castle and found the smashed wooden doors. They knocked at the iron one. 'Wudei'a, Wudei'a, let us in. What has happened?' Their sister let them in and told them everything that had happened since she had eaten the broad bean.

'And I'm sure the demon will come back tonight and break through the iron door,' Wudei'a said.

'We shall be ready for him,' said the brothers.

They dug a pit inside the room and filled it with hot coals. Then they stretched a soft woven carpet over their trap and waited.

That night the demon came back and sang outside Wudei'a's door.

Don't commit a second sin.
Let your poor old father in.

And this time Wudei'a replied:

My father bids me here to bide.
You may sit and rot outside.

The demon was so furious that, with a mighty roar, he broke the iron door down. The brothers were waiting for him. 'Sit down, friend,' they said, 'and join us.' They pointed to the comfortable carpet and the demon tried to sit down, but of course he fell right into the pit. The brothers piled wood on top of him until he was quite burned up. The only bit of him that was left behind was one of his nails, which lay on the floor.

Later, when Wudei'a was tidying up, she pricked her finger on this nail and a splinter of it went under her skin. She fell down dead on the spot.

Her brothers found her and grieved for the sister they had known for such a short time. They dressed her in her most beautiful robe and tied her to the camel on which she had arrived.

'Run through the desert and take her back to our father's house,' they said to the camel.

As the camel ran through the desert, it was captured by thieves. They were amazed to find a beautiful girl's body on it, but that didn't stop them from trying to steal an emerald ring off her finger. But as the ring was being pulled off, it dislodged the sliver of the demon's nail from under Wudei'a's skin.

She sat up and stretched her arms wide.

'What a good sleep I've had,' she said. 'But who are you? And why am I tied to the camel?'

The thieves ran away terrified and Wudei'a made the camel take her back to the castle.

Her brothers were overjoyed to see her! They all decided to return to their parents' home. Each brother rode a horse and Wudei'a travelled on the camel.

'Look, I have brought back your seven sons,' she called out when they reached their parents' house.

Then there was feasting and celebrating such as you have never seen. Everyone in the village came, except the aunt, who was never heard of again. And the brothers and their sister lived at their parents' home ever afterwards.

But what we don't know is whether Wudei'a's name was changed to a new one, meaning 'the girl who brought back seven'. I think it should have been — do you?

ACHOL AND MAPER

S U D A N E S E

Maper was a big brother and his little sister was called Achol. Their father had three older sons by his first wife and they all lived in a camp in the heart of lion country.

When Achol was still a tiny girl, her family had a piece of luck. She was betrothed to a rich man called Kwol, who had lots of cattle. She would marry Kwol when she was a grown woman, and she would grow up never wanting for anything.

Well, this made her half-brothers very jealous. 'Why should Achol be rich and not us?' they asked. 'She isn't even our mother's daughter. She will favour her full-brother, who carries her round on his back.' They decided to get rid of Achol and Maper at once.

Their chance came when their father told them to take their cattle to a new grazing ground, far from the village. 'Take your little brother and sister with you,' said the father. 'It will be an adventure for them.' When they made camp on the first night of

48

their journey, the half-brothers put a sleeping-draught into the bedtime milk of little Achol and in Maper's, too.

When the children woke up next morning, the camp had moved on and they were all alone. There was a gourd of milk left beside them, but no sign of their big brothers.

They had no idea where to go or what to do, so they drank the milk and sheltered in a ditch made by elephants. As the sun rose higher in the sky, the children slept, and along came a lioness. She looked down over the edge of the ditch and the children woke up to see the tawny eyes of the lioness gazing into theirs.

'We're dead!' cried the children. 'We're going to be eaten!'

But the lioness could speak, so she said, 'Don't cry. I shan't eat you. Whose children are you? Are you the children of humans?'

'Yes, we are,' they said, still trembling with fear.

'Then how were you abandoned here?' asked the lioness.

'Our half-brothers left us behind,' said Maper.

'Deliberately,' added Achol.

'Come with me,' said the lioness. 'I'll look after you. I have no cubs, so I'd like to take care of you.'

The children went with her, but Maper didn't really trust her. After a while, he managed to run away. He meant to come back and rescue his sister but, although he was able to meet up with the rest of his family, Maper could never find where the lioness had taken Achol.

Many years passed and Maper believed that his sister was dead. But the lioness had been true to her word. She looked after Achol as if she had been her real lion-daughter. The lioness hunted other animals and brought back fresh meat every day. In time, Achol learned to make fire and cook her food and she was very fond of her lioness-mother.

Achol made a hut for them to live in and kept house for her new mother. And so they lived happily until Achol was a grown woman.

At this time, Maper and his brothers again moved their cattle into lion country. Of course, he had told his parents what the brothers had done to him and his sister but they had denied it. It was a long time ago and the big brothers were no longer jealous of Maper.

One day, when Maper was herding cattle with friends his own age, they strayed near to the lioness's house. Achol was sitting outside the entrance but they didn't recognise each other. One of his friends was thirsty and called out to Achol, 'Girl, give us water!'

'This is a dangerous watering-hole for humans,' said Achol. 'You must not stay long.' But she gave them water all the same. When they had quenched their thirst, the young men left.

Shortly afterwards, the lioness returned, dragging a plump young antelope in her jaws. She dropped it outside the hut and sang to Achol, as she always did:

Mother's home now, little daughter.
Make the fire and heat the water.
Achol never shall get thinner
While a lion brings her dinner.
Come and kiss your loving mother
Who loves you more than any other.

Achol came out and embraced the lioness, planting kisses on her broad nose. Then she cooked their dinner and told the lioness about the young men who had come and asked for water.

'You must get married some day,' said the lioness. 'It is good for you to meet young human men. If they come again, be nice to them, but don't tell them that your mother is a lion.'

Although Maper hadn't recognised Achol, he couldn't forget the girl outside the hut. He went back to look for her the next day, taking his friend with him. On the way there they both talked about how beautiful the girl had been.

As they reached the hut, Maper said, 'I have such a strong feeling about that girl. Perhaps it means I should marry her?'

A lizard on the wall of the hut said, 'That man wants to marry his sister!'

Maper was astonished. 'I have no sister,' he told his friend.

The roof-beams of the hut groaned, 'That man wants to marry his sister!'

'I used to have a sister,' said Maper doubtfully.

The grass of the hut whispered, 'That man wantsss to marry hiss sissster!'

'Could it be...?' asked Maper.

Just then, the girl came out of the hut.

'Girl,' said Maper. 'Who are you?'

'I am called Achol,' said the girl.

Maper clasped her in his arms. 'I am Maper, your brother,' he cried. 'And I have searched for you ever since the lioness took you!'

How happy they were to find each other again. Maper introduced his friend to Achol and then asked her to come back to his camp with them.

'Oh, but I can't leave the lioness, my mother,' said Achol. 'She would be so lonely without me.'

'But it is better for you to live with your own kind,' said Maper. 'And think how your real mother has missed you — and your father too.'

Achol remembered what the lioness had said about meeting humans. So in the end she was persuaded and went with the young men to their camp.

That evening the lioness came back to the hut, with more fresh meat. Outside she sang her usual song:

Mother's home now, little daughter.
Make the fire and heat the water.
Achol never shall get thinner
While a lion brings her dinner.
Come and kiss your loving mother
Who loves you more than any other.

But there was no reply. Over and over the lioness repeated her song. In the end she went into the hut and found it empty. Leaving her meal behind, she bounded along the trail, following the still-fresh scent of her human daughter.

Achol was welcomed back to her family with great joy. They were amazed that she had been looked after so gently by a lioness.

By evening, that same lioness had reached the village where the cattle-herders were living. Cautiously, she circled the village,

picking out Achol's scent from among all the other human beings. When she reached what she hoped was the right hut, the lioness sang softly:

Come and kiss your loving mother
Who loves you more than any other.

Achol heard her voice and ran out of the hut. 'Mother, Mother! I am so pleased to see you!' she cried.

The villagers came running to see what the commotion was. Achol's father killed a bull in the lioness's honour and invited her to sit down and eat with them. Achol told her mother that she was going to marry Maper's friend — for old Kwol had died long ago — and the lioness decided to stay and live among the humans.

She never had to hunt again as the villagers provided her with enough food from their cattle. And when Achol got married, the lioness moved in with her and her husband. When their children were born she helped to look after them as tenderly as if they had been her own grandcubs.

TRAMPLING THE DEMONS

JAPANESE

One day a sister and brother went up to the hills to gather chestnuts. It was a mild autumn day and the nuts were plentiful. The brother and sister wandered apart, gathering nuts, and were soon out of sight and sound of one another.

When the boy's baskets were full, he came back to where he had left his sister. He wasn't too worried; after all, he had strayed far away himself. But when he found her scarf caught on the branches of a tree, he did become alarmed.

He searched further and further in the hills until he came to a big house standing all on its own. Outside were two tall purple pillars and a purple gate between them. On one of the pillars hung a piece of bright cloth, which the boy recognised as a fragment of his sister's dress.

He was very afraid by now, but he thought, 'Whoever has my sister must have taken her in through this gate. I have to try to rescue her.'

As he approached closer, the boy saw that guarding the gate was a purple demon. The boy was hidden behind a bush, so the demon hadn't seen him, but the boy couldn't think how he was going to get past safely. Then the demon gave a great yawn and curled up in front of the gate and went to sleep. The boy summoned up all his courage and crept forward on tiptoe. Cautiously, he stepped over the demon, but careful as he was, he managed to step on one of the demon's feet.

The purple demon muttered in his sleep, 'Curse these field mice scampering over my foot. They keep me awake.'

The boy was very scared, but the demon didn't wake up. So he crept on. He didn't seem to be getting any closer to the house when he came to a green gate, guarded by a green demon. It wasn't long before that one, too, stretched out to sleep and was soon snoring loudly.

The boy's heart was in his mouth as he crept past this second demon. Again, he trod on the demon's foot as he passed. 'Wretched field mice!' muttered the green demon. 'How is anyone to sleep with them skittering about the place?' But he didn't see the boy.

The boy walked on and came to a red gate and guess what was guarding it! Yes, a red demon, bigger than the other two and fiercer looking. But that one also got drowsy and lay down to sleep.

'Luck comes in threes,' thought the boy. 'I hope my luck holds. Here goes!' And he crept past the red demon and through the red gate, but again he stepped on the demon's foot. The demon stirred. 'What a nuisance these field mice are!' he mumbled. 'Always scurrying over me when I'm trying to sleep.'

The boy couldn't believe his luck, but now he saw that he had reached the house. Outside the front door were a pair of straw sandals he recognised — his sister's! That gave him courage. He called to his sister and she came out.

How happy they were to see one another! But they were both still in terrible danger. The chief demon lived in the house, but he had gone out.

'He will be back soon and, if he finds you, he's sure to eat you,' said the girl as they entered the house. Just then they heard the sound of a mighty demon harumphing outside the front door.

'Quick,' said the girl. 'Hide inside this bamboo trunk.'

So her brother hid himself and in came the demon, as blue as blue can be. He stood in front of the hearth warming himself by the fire. Then he sniffed the air.

'Girl, I smell a human being. And I mean another one, not you.'

'There's nobody here but me, sir,' said the girl.

The demon didn't believe her and he roamed around the room until he noticed a bit of the boy's sash sticking out of the trunk.

'What's this?' he roared, and he threw open the lid and dragged out the trembling boy.

'Oh, please don't hurt him,' begged the girl. 'He's my brother.'

But the demon just laughed, showing all his teeth.

'We'll have a contest,' said the blue demon. 'If your brother wins,

he is safe. If I win — which I will — I shall eat him!'

It was supper-time and the demon's idea was to have a competition to see who could eat a bowl of boiled rice the quickest. The girl filled two bowls with rice, but she managed to fit a smaller bowl inside her brother's so that it held far less rice than it seemed.

The boy was rather hungry after all that nut-gathering and his adventures with the demons so he won easily. The demon was furious.

'Best of three!' he roared. 'We'll have another contest — eating beans this time.'

Fortunately for the children, the demon was rather short-sighted and he didn't notice that while the girl served her brother real beans, she gave the demon pebbles to eat instead. The boy won again.

'Hmm,' said the demon, rubbing his belly, which felt very uncomfortable after all that rice followed by pebbles. 'We'll go to sleep now and in the morning we'll have a new kind of contest, cutting down trees. Whoever cuts down a tree first wins. And the loser is eaten!'

With that, he lay down to sleep, groaning. It was all very unfair, because the boy had already won twice and, besides, he couldn't have eaten the demon even if he had wanted to. But such contests usually are unfair when a demon is involved.

In the night, the girl sharpened a hatchet for her brother to use, but she blunted the demon's hatchet with a stone. In the morning, she called the demon early and said, 'Time to get up and cut trees!'

The demon and the boy each chose a tree and took up their hatchets. The boy's tree was soon lying on the ground while the demon's hatchet kept bouncing off the trunk. The demon was very frustrated because he wanted to eat the boy — and the girl, too!

'Now's your chance,' the girl told her brother.

He crept up behind the demon as he struggled with the tree and whacked off his head with his hatchet. The demon fell down dead at the foot of the tree.

Then all the other demons — the purple, the green and the red — came and knelt down in front of the boy and girl. They could have eaten them but they didn't, because the children had killed the demon chief.

The house was full of treasure — gold and silver coins, emerald and diamond necklaces, sapphire tiaras and ruby bracelets. All these were loaded into bamboo trunks like the one the boy had hidden in and the demons carried them to the children's home.

And so the boy and girl who had gone out to gather chestnuts came home with chests of treasure instead. Imagine how surprised and pleased their parents were!

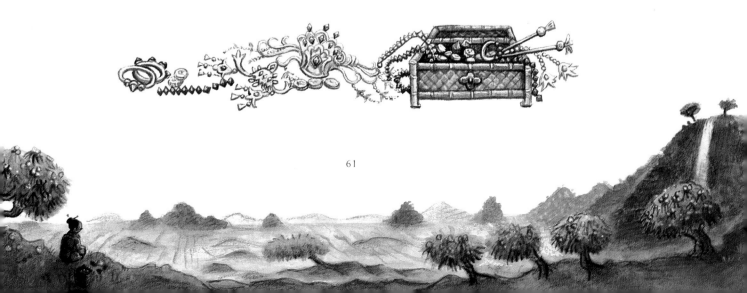

SOURCES

Hansel and Gretel

This is the best known of all the brother and sister stories. Surprisingly, the Brothers Grimm don't mention gingerbread in describing the witch's house, but it is so much part of the tradition that I have kept it in, and added other goodies in its construction.
Grimm, J. and W., *Grimms' Fairy Tales*, 1812–15.

The Quillwork Girl and her Seven Star Brothers

This is unusual among North American stories in portraying the buffalo as the enemy.
Erdoes, R. and Ortiz, A. (eds.), *American Indian Myths and Legends*, Pantheon Books, New York, 1984.

The Red Cow

There are obvious parallels at the end of the story with Cinderella. In the original, the stepmother and stepdaughter are killed by being tied to wild stallions.
Downing, C., *Armenian Folk-Tales and Fables*, Oxford University Press, Oxford, 1972 (recorded in 1914).

Alionushka and Ivanushka

There is also a version of this story in *Grimms' Fairy Tales*, called simply 'Brother and Sister', in which the children are not royal. It is from this version that I have taken the happy conversion of the kid-brother to his human form. Afanas'ev, A., (trans. by Guterman, N.), *Russian Fairy Tales*, Pantheon, New York, 1973.

The Girl who Banished Seven Brothers

I have toned down some of the violence from the original. The desert-demon in that is described as a ghoul and makes Wudei'a pay for her fire with a strip of her own skin. It is her blood-trail that the demon follows to the castle. Carter, A. (ed.), *The Virago Book of Fairy Tales*, Virago Press, London, 1991. Carter gives her source as Bushnaq, I. (ed.) *Arab Folktales*, Penguin Books, London, 1987.

Achol and Maper

I have played down the incest-motif of the original.
Carter, A. (ed.), *The Second Virago Book of Fairy Tales*, Virago Press, London, 1992. Carter gives her source as Deng, F. M., *Dinka Folktales, African Stories from Sudan*, Holmes and Meier, New York, 1974.

Trampling the Demons

I am grateful to Samira Kirollos for locating this tale.
Hagin-Mayer, F. (ed. and trans.), *Ancient Tales in Modern Japan — An Anthology of Japanese Folktales*, 1899, reprinted by the Indiana University Press, Indianapolis, 1984